THIS BOOK BELONGS TO

I0620927

An A-Girl Studio book
published 2015 in the USA.

For additional information, please contact:
A-Girl Studio
P.O. Box 213, Burbank, CA 91503 U.S.A.
www.a-girlstudio.com

ISBN: 978-1-936622-31-3

First paperback edition, 2015

The Wrecking Faerie

Volume 1

By
Elizabeth Watasin

A-GIRL STUDIO

CHAPTER ONE

WHERE have all the monsters gone?

On the shrouded edges of the Earth, far from the everyday and mundane, the Twilight World lay, ancient haven to the magical and monstrous. Ghost ships flew over midnight oceans, and forgotten kingdoms rose and fell, hidden in valleys or atop high mountains. Creatures roamed the forests, and in the modest yet modern towns that dotted the forest interior, Other-beings lived and worked.

In one such town, called Little Salem, the nights belonged to their wild children. Right then, raucous teens raised hell around a bonfire on the Enchanting Forest's fringes. Motorcycles roared, and their leather-clad riders whooped. Tail pipes rumbled and spewed, to the dismay of watching, ancient neighbors.

Three females of the faerie-kind lounged, hidden by the forest, and viewed the rambunctious display.

"Ugh, diesel," the eldest commented. She was crowned in ivy and wore a golden girdle on her hips.

"Must they burn such things in their loud machines?" the second eldest said.

"Their silly machines annoy me so!" the youngest exclaimed, and she wore plumeria blossoms in her long hair.

The eldest smiled down at her faerie sisters. "Yet they are mere noise. They can do no harm to such as we."

"Certainly! We are faeries of the Court," the youngest said, smug. "They are mere children, behind our ken."

"No comparison," the middle faerie added and laughed.

The foliage rustled, and a fourth faerie burst through.

"Hush! Our dark sister approaches!" she warned.

The faeries scattered, fleeing deeper into the forest. Leaves stirred in their wake. A bared foot landed on the forest floor the faeries had deserted.

Two winged sprites looked on, clinging to a bush's branches.

"Ha! What can startle the *mighty* Daughters of the Court so?" one asked the other.

"Their dark sister, of course!" the other replied.

"Afraid she'll add 'em ta her long list o' conquests, yeah?"

The sprites burst into loud laughter and flew away.

Fairer Than the Fairest of all Faeries stepped forwards, flanked by more sprites, circling and smirking. Small white flowers dotted her tumble of thick red hair, and around her hips, a gold girdle hung, heavy with medallions and large canine teeth. Her heavy-lidded gaze slid to what her fellow faeries had been watching. A pretty girl's platinum blonde hair shined in the bonfire light. Fairer Than turned to face the fire and rested a forearm against a tree.

⇜

Bunny Baker, good teen witch, and her greaser girl-friend, the vampire Dean, ignored the rowdiness, eyes only for each other. Bunny was seventeen and a daughter of a seventh daughter, who right then had only adoring eyes for her sweetheart. They'd met at one of Spooky's cemetery fests, where Dean had rode in with her motor-cycle gang. Wearing a leather jacket, dungarees, and mo-torcycle boots, Dean sported a slicked-back ducktail and a fanged grin that made Bunny's heart thump. When young warlocks picked a fight and rioting ensued, Bunny chose to side with Dean. As a result, she'd forgotten that she'd gone to Spooky's hoping to meet a faerie girl. She gained a wickedly sweet vampire, instead.

"Dean, do you have to go to the vampire's ball tomor-row night?" Bunny pouted as she leaned against her girl-friend and her bike. "I want you to come to the Queer Youth meeting with me."

"Baby, I can't, and believe me, I've tried to get out of it." Dean grinned, a toothpick between her teeth. "Why don't you come to the ball with me?"

"Sure." Bunny smiled. "Only if you wear the ball gown."

Dean reached up and plucked Bunny's pointed witch hat from her head. Bunny pulled Dean's toothpick from her mouth.

"Hey," Dean said. She brought Bunny around to press her back against her front.

"I'll pass," Bunny said as she enjoyed Dean's embrace. She put the toothpick to her own mouth. "I don't want to

be the first witch ever to crash the vampires' most exclu-
sive, biggest bash in Little Salem. They may tear a girl like
me into little pieces."

"Naw, werewolves do that sort of thing," Dean assured.
"Vampires know how to treat a pretty witch."

Bunny turned and looked up at Dean from beneath her
lashes. "Now do they?"

"I believe I'm an authority on that subject."

"I guess I'll be all right by myself at Q-Youth," Bunny
sighed.

"I'm missing you already, Bunny," Dean said.

They kissed.

⁓

Mugg, the punk sprite, hovered near the oblivious
couple, beating his ragged wings. Wearing leather pants
and steel-toed boots, he idly scratched the elbow of his tattooed arm, wondering when the kissing would end. The
kids' discussion, he decided, was over for the time being.
He flew back to the forest and to his mistress, his mohawk
fluttering.

⁓

Fairer Than watched the blonde witch speak to her
love interest, a vampire both androgynous and rebellious
in appearance. Outlined by firelight, the witch's curves
were evident in a mid-length pencil skirt with blouse and
short-sleeved jacket, her pointed hat still in the vampire's
grip. On the girl's neck was a small bandage, covering a
vampire's bite.

Fairer Than stared at the platinum shine of the girl's locks, its length just off the shoulder. A curling wave of hair fell to the side of the girl's warm and receptive, hazel-eyed gaze.

Mugg zipped across the clearing, bypassing boisterous bikers. He alighted on Fairer Than's shoulder.

"Her name is Bunny," he whispered.

The corner of Fairer Than's mouth crept up.

"Lovely," she said.

CHAPTER TWO

The next night, while Dean attended the Vampire's Ball, Bunny changed out of her outfit for school into something more appropriate for socializing. Little Salem sat by a lake—known to inhabitants as "The Lady's Lake"—which harbored a little wetland on one shore. In that swamp, beneath cypress trees and hanging vines, Q-Youth of Little Salem held its meet-and-greet.

The night being mild, Bunny entered the moonlit Okonee Swamp campground wearing a sheath dress of ivory, her black flats matching her black hat. Out on the lake, a prehistoric dinosaur's silhouette glided along the water's surface, then submerged from view. Bunny looked around at the circle of log benches where people were already gathered, some of whom she recognized from school. Sally, the living apple doll, was coordinator, and she was already chatting with a crew-cut mummy girl who was obviously interested in her. Bunny wandered near the refreshments table. Fausta leaned elbows on it, as if waiting to serve someone punch, but Bunny doubted the devil girl intended to help with anything.

"Hiya Bunny," she said. She smiled, revealing a gap in her front teeth. "Nice ta see ya bringing your goody self.'"

"Hi Fausta," Bunny greeted, cool. She was glad to not see a dark witch in attendance; she wasn't interested in a confrontation. The party planner in her eyed the table's layout. The pitcher of punch held skull ice cubes, and a large black spider sat in the chips bowl Fausta was helping herself to.

"Free after the meeting?" Fausta casually inquired. "I'll treat ya to soda at the shop." Fausta wore a tight pullover sweater along with a tight pencil skirt, her black hair in a perfect flip. She gave Bunny a sardonic look. "Is that expression on your face a 'no'? I don't see the vampire around."

"Fausta, I know as a devil girl you have to try stuff, but it's annoying." Bunny turned to go. Fausta suddenly rose and leaned her hip and a hand on the table.

"Did you know? I'm part-faerie," she enticed.

Bunny looked at her in amazement. "No, you're not."

"Yes, I am."

"No, you're—Fausta, why are you telling me this?"

Fausta leaned close, startling Bunny by the sudden proximity. "I heard ya like faeries. Wanna see my wings?"

Bunny drew her wand.

"*Beat it, dematerialize,*" she incanted, swinging her wand up, and Fausta disappeared within a flashing eruption of sparkling smoke. A shriek sounded out on the lake as Fausta reappeared in the air above. She plummeted and hit the water with a loud splash.

"Creep," Bunny exclaimed.

"Hey, Bunny," a female voice called from the tree branches above.

"Yeah, hey Bunny," another female voice greeted, and the two snickered.

Bunny looked up, spying two cat girls nestled in the tree. They looked down in amusement. Their cat faces bore forehead markings and they wore brightly colored barrettes. As they giggled, their small fangs showed.

"Hi Nix, Pix," Bunny said, wary.

"You came all by yourself to your first Q-Youth meeting, really?" Nix said.

"Or maybe she's here to do some fishing?" Pix said to Nix. "See what's here biting?" They broke into peals of laughter.

Bunny swung her wand down.

"Beat it, dematerialize!" Bunny incanted, incensed. Nix and Pix disappeared in a puff of sparkling smoke. Two more shrieks sounded over the water.

"Ha!" Bunny said, and snapped her fingers. Sending teasing girls into the lake might be over-kill, but Bunny had learned one thing fast and early while growing up in Little Salem: it was best to show Other-beings that she wasn't a human to push around. She stepped to return to the campground.

"Lovely trick, from a lovely witch," a woman said behind her. The rich tone was deep and sultry.

"Beat it," Bunny said, raising her wand. She turned.

Her incantation died on her lips. A tall faerie stood before her, leaning a forearm on a tree. Her thick, red tresses were dotted with tiny white flowers, the locks gathered and held by one gold ring. Her curvaceous body was clad in a deep green kirtle with a brief bodice, loosely laced over her breasts. The kirtle's straps had fallen from her broad shoulders and hung, ragged. One draped a gold armband circling a bicep. Old-gold medallions and large, sharp teeth made up the faerie's heavy girdle, and beneath her skirt's rough hem, her bare toes poked. The faerie stepped away from the tree.

"I'm Fairer Than," she said.

"I'm…Bunny." Fairer Than approached, and Bunny could think of nothing else to say. As the faerie neared, the green irises of her heavy-lidded gaze became evident, and her pouty-lipped mouth curled into a smile.

"Charmed," she said.

Fairer Than continued past Bunny and slowly circled. "This is my first meeting. And you?" she asked.

"It's—it's mine too." Bunny held her wand close as Fairer Than stepped around her. "I didn't know the faerie came to these meetings."

"I'm unlike other faerie," Fairer Than said low at Bunny's shoulder. She stopped to stand beside Bunny.

"Look." Fairer Than nodded to the campground clearing where the others took seats around a fire. "It's starting. Can we sit together?"

Bunny didn't think that was a good idea.

"Sure," Bunny said. Fairer Than's scent distracted— flowery and earthy, resinous and creamy. The faerie's skin exuded heat. Somewhere in the very back of Bunny's mind, she knew she was forgetting something.

They found a log to sit on as Sally opened the meeting, the mummy girl front and center and attentive. Fausta plopped down on a log, soaked, while Pix and Nix dragged themselves out of the water. They bewailed their wet state, but no one paid heed.

Fausta looked over at Bunny and Fairer Than while wringing her hair, and to Bunny's relief, she remained silent. The devil girl stared wide-eyed at Fairer Than.

Fairer Than, in the full light of the fire, looked like a fully developed woman out of the Arthurian legends, someone almost too sophisticated for such a youthful gathering. But the appearances of faeries could be deceptive. Bunny tried to remind herself of that.

Far across town, at a great banquet hall, resplendent
vampires gathered. From undead kings to countesses,
rock stars to unblinking monsters, every manner of vampire present in the Twilight World were in attendance.
Three vampire girls from three different eras ran through
the crowd. The first wore a Goth dress of slinky black,
the second an embroidered velvet tunic, and the last girl
followed in a hooped ball gown, her hair in bouncing sau-
sage curls.

"Dean! Dean!" they called as they pushed by partygo-
ers. "Dean!"

Dean appeared behind them as the girls pressed on.

"Ha!" Dean said, toothpick in her mouth. Not only did
she lose the fawning girls, but her own dress jacket too,
and stood then in waistcoat and shirtsleeves, her bow tie
undone.

"*Yu Ying*! Stop playing with the girls and come with
me!" her father cried behind her.

Dean shrieked. Nothing could startle her more than
the voice of her father, Zongxiang Lingbo Zhuofan Shao
Shang Yu, Golden Bloody Overlord of the One Thou-
sand Vampire Horde. He was possibly the most decrepit
looking of the ancient vampires present, his frail bones
clad in embroidered silk robes. His visage, with its scrag-
gly long mustache, frightened even his own children. He
took hold of Dean's ear and pulled her along as his tall hat
bobbed in the crowd. Being a very stiff, living corpse, he
did not walk but hopped.

"Pop! Call me Dean!"

Shang Yu chortled and pulled more.

"Yeah-yeah! Some other time," he dismissed. He

hopped to a stop before a small woman with a slicked bob, her plump body sheathed in a dress draped with pearls. Shang Yu stood Dean before her.

"Baroness Von Blaud," Shang Yu addressed. "May I present to you my number one daughter and son, Yu Ying! She will succeed me and lead my vampire horde."

Dean wanted to protest. She wasn't 'number one' daughter or son; she had three sisters ahead of her. It also wasn't her fault that her brothers had tried to kill Shang Yu, making her the chosen "son."

The baroness raised a jeweled lorgnette and stared up at Dean, her narrow gaze baleful.

"Charmed," the baroness said coldly, and inspected Dean more.

"Baroness Von Blaud, don't you have a daughter?" Shang Yu suddenly inquired, and prodded Dean even closer to the woman.

Dean wished then that Bunny were present so she could dematerialize the woman.

After more cool formalities, Dean made her desperate escape into the crowd. But not before her father had succeeded, as he usually did, in making his heir-apparent miserable. She did not want to think about other people's daughters.

"I just want to be with Bunny," Dean said.

CHAPTER THREE

Little Salem's living rooster skeleton filled its non-existent lungs and crowed, accompanying the sunrise. Kids gathered at Shivers, the burger and soda shop, and ate breakfast before heading to school. A gorgon girl sat in a booth with her mummy boyfriend in his letter jacket. A reanimated monster boy chatted with a freckled Cyclops girl and her friend, a fish girl. Across the checkered tile floor, Dean stood by as Bunny enjoyed an orange juice at the steel topped and chrome counter. Books and witch's hat set aside, Bunny had already drunk her warmed milk whipped with two raw eggs—her breakfast staple. She laughed as Dean regaled her with tales of the vampires' ball.

"Liked it that much, huh?" Bunny said, smiling.

"Next time, enchant a frog to take my place." Dean soaked in Bunny's presence, thinking her warmth and smile easily obliterated the ill effects of being around snooty, old, and very cold vampires. "How was your first Q-Youth meeting?"

"It was okay. Sally worked hard putting it together.

They're planning a mixer." Bunny looked up at her. "It'll be a dance. And I happened to meet someone—"

"Dean!" Her vampire buddy Cesar called from the glass entrance door. "Auto shop's open! Let's go!"

Dean gave Bunny a quick kiss on the head. If anything could pull her away from Bunny, it was cars. "Sorry, Bunny, gotta go. See you tonight?"

"Won't miss it," Bunny said. Dean headed for the door, eager to start her day with an engine.

⤚

Bunny put the straw of her orange carton to her smiling lips and watched Dean leave just as her own friends, Blanchet and Pippita entered. Though Bunny was born to the Twilight World and followed the culture she grew up in—one with soda shops, hot rods, and pencil skirts—some came to Little Salem from different eras and places. Whether it was a two thousand-year-old mummy or a spacefaring extraterrestrial, the Twilight World was haven to all migrating Other-beings. Blanchet's family had immigrated from a time period later than Bunny's known world, one filled with technology and advancements Bunny couldn't envision.

"Think of it as yourself having to go back to a period with no television or cars," Blanchet had once said to her. "Like the medieval period."

"I enjoy the medieval kingdoms here," Bunny had said. "My aunties and I like to enter the cooking competitions."

Blanchet had thanked her for that information, believing that she herself was not ready for any medieval sightseeing.

Blanchet waved, tall and thin in a black mini skirt, white dress shirt and black tie, a tiny top hat atop her massive afro. Bunny and Blanchet's magical practices couldn't be more different, but Bunny considered Blanchet a valued colleague and friend. Anyone could see that Blanchet was on her way to university and becoming a respectable witch doctor, once they graduated Haunt High.

Pippita, on the other hand, was a compact and fully packed little red demon with a temper to match. She was always ready to stir trouble and revel in the chaos resulting. Bunny didn't know why she tolerated her childhood friend's amity—if it could be called that. As Bunny's aunties had said to her, better to keep a mischievous imp close rather than have her working her tricks from afar.

"So how was the Q-Youth meeting?" Blanchet greeted as she laid her books on the counter beside Bunny. "Meet any new people?"

"Yeah, like any *devil girls*?" Pippita called from the stool she'd hopped into next to Blanchet. Bunny gave her a look and then ignored her.

"Get this," Bunny enthused to Blanchet. "I met an actual *faerie daughter* of the Court last night! Is that wild?"

"Git outta here," Pippita exclaimed. "She must've been slummin'!"

"Thanks a lot for telling Fausta what I supposedly like, Pippita," Bunny added coldly. "How much did she pay you, anyway?"

"Haw!" Pippita guffawed, her forked tongue protruding, and downed a packet of Bang! Rocks Candy the soda jerk had given her. He then laid a bowl of Sparkle Flakes before Blanchet with a carton of milk. Both were the girls' usual breakfast orders. Blanchet added her milk, causing her cereal to sparkle.

"You have to admit, Bunny, you were really into faerie girls before you met Dean," she remarked.

"Obsessed," Pippita added, her mouth emitting tiny,

colorful explosions.

"Okay, yes, I was." Bunny leaned on a hand and sighed. "But that was me, dreaming. Meeting this faerie really made it clear to me; they are beyond our ken."

The glass entrance slammed open.

Fairer Than stepped inside, her red hair riotous. Flanked by hovering sprites, her heavy-lidded gaze traveled around the diner's staring occupants. Her regard came to rest on Bunny.

Bunny froze on her stool. Fairer Than approached.

"Hello, Bunny," she said, her languid attention warm. Two goblins peered from behind Fairer Than's skirts, one tattooed with pierced ears and the other buck-toothed and wearing a knit cap. The sprites circled.

"Wha—what'll you have?" the soda jerk said to Fairer Than.

She looked at the nervous young man, seemingly surprised by the interruption. A sprite landed on his white hat.

"Do you…have mist cakes?" Fairer Than asked.

"No."

"Pity." She glanced over to Bunny, who still hadn't found her voice. Fairer Than reached into her bodice front.

She drew out a hard pack of cigarettes and flicked it, a single cigarette popping out. She put it to her lips and drew it from the pack.

Foooosh! The cigarette's end flared, a tiny inferno, and then subsided. Sounds of awe rose in the diner as Bunny stared at Fairer Than's pursed lips.

Faeries didn't smoke, nor was summoning fire by sheer will easy. Fairer Than had done it without any magical aid.

"Miss! You can't smoke in here. Sorry, but you gotta leave." The soda jerk's hat fell forwards into his face, the sprite pushing it down. The tattooed goblin, having gained a stool, reached over and pulled hard on the young man's bow tie.

Fairer Than returned her pack to her bosom and touched her hair as she stood next to Bunny. Her other hand came to rest at her hip. Bunny remained tongue-tied and looked aside. Fairer Than exhaled smoke.

"Sure," she said, cigarette dangling from her lips, and Bunny returned her gaze to Fairer Than. The faerie leaned over and smiled.

"Nice seeing you, Bunny," she said.

Fairer Than turned and exited, the door slamming open again. Bunny watched Fairer Than's behind move, a motion strong enough to wreck any approaching. The goblins stuck out their tongues at the diner crowd before following.

Once the faerie and her kin had departed, exclamations erupted.

"I didn't know faeries smoked," Blanchet said.

"Yeah! That is one *baaaaaad* faerie!" Pippita crowed.

"She lit dat *spontaneously*," monster boy said, "just like da demons do!"

"Maybe she's one of them elemental, woodsy folk?" Cyclops girl suggested, highly amused. Bunny noticed the gorgon girl, Madeline, leaving in a huff as Scott, her mummy boyfriend protested.

"Hey Bunny! Is *that* the faerie you met last night?" Pippita yelled.

"Let's go to class," Bunny said, curt, and retrieved her witch's hat. She dismounted while Blanchet grinned. Pippita took hold of her cloven hooves and spun on her stool.

"Wow," Pippita crowed. "What a *babe*! And is she baaaaaad!" She hopped down and called to Blanchet as she and Bunny exited.

"Hell, Blanchet, if I were gay—" Pippita said.

"Pippita, let's go!" Bunny yelled outside the diner. She turned for school. Fairer Than and her faerie folk were nowhere to be seen.

Bunny sighed. The morning light seemed weaker in its beauty, as if something were missing.

Haunt High's clock tower gonged, and the school day began.

Though Bunny liked learning well enough (however, as a witch, practicing one's craft or personal powers was more interesting than general education, just as it was for the mermaids, werewolves, and mad scientists), her ability to concentrate seemed to flee her that day. Every question asked of her produced one inexplicable answer.

"And who can tell me which herb is used with the concoction we're working on today?" the teacher asked Bunny's biology and brew lab. "Hemlock or henbane? Bunny?"

Bunny looked up from her caldron, her apron a splattered mess. "Fairer Than," she answered.

In history class, the teacher droned as Bunny attempted to take notes, monster boy dozing in the seat beside her while Nix and Pix sat in back and nuzzled noses. Bunny looked at her notepaper. She'd written *Fairer Than* repeatedly.

"Sooooo," the teacher said at his lecturing podium. "According to *this* lore, the warrior goddess is made up of three aspects. Who can name one? Bunny?"

Bunny stared. "Fairer Than."

"Fairer Than—Fairer Than—Fairer Than! I cannot get her out of my mind!" Bunny held her head. "I must be under a spell!" It was lunch break, and Blanchet stood with Bunny in the girls' bathroom. Blanchet paused in working on her afro and stared in concern at her friend.

She stuck her hair pick back in her hair. "Bunny, a spell of bewitchment could be anything. There are too many variations and styles. We're also talking about faerie magic." She thought a moment. "I need to order faerie books." She pulled out her pocket journal and retractable pen from her skirt's pocket, mumbling something about wishing she still had her phone.

"I nearly think it's not a spell," Bunny said. "All Fairer Than has done is *look* at me."

Blanchet glanced up from her notebook. "We could do a casting to see what's sticking to you."

Bunny shook her head. "That's a complex spell. Until we're powerful witches, we can't do it faster. And I don't think I can wait until after school. I'm already wrecked by what's happening."

"It's times like this that I miss having digital technology," Blanchet mused. "I could have searched for a faerie beguiling right away on my ph—"

"Blanchet! That's not helping." Whenever Blanchet talked about her "technology," Bunny could not follow. Anything beyond a television set or a princess phone was incomprehensible.

The bell rang.

"I'll-I'll figure it out," Bunny assured Blanchet, and they left the bathroom.

But once in her math class, Bunny's mind was distracted by Fairer Than's face.

Hello, Bunny.

Hello, Bunny.

Bunny. Bunny.

"Mr Wretched?" Bunny raised her hand, addressing the ghoul writing on the chalkboard. "May I be excused for a moment?"

Outside on the school grounds, Bunny crept behind the hedge, avoiding the detection of a teacher or monitor. She'd retrieved her witch's hat and broom. There was only one thing she could do.

Bunny ran and then leapt onto the broom's stick, seating herself sidesaddle. She and the broom lifted, leaving gravity and ground behind. She soared for the sky.

Enchanting Forest lay before her, and the foreboding, bent peak of Witch Hat Mountain. Bunny pointed her broomstick for where she believed Fairer Than might be.

CHAPTER FOUR

In a forest clearing not far from Little Salem and The Lady's Lake, Bunny landed. Though the great trees of the Enchanting Forest could be foreboding, and its faerie inhabitants mischievous and (at times) deadly, Bunny had always thought of it as home. The Goddess was best understood in the forest. The females of the faerie kind had seemed like one aspect of that which Bunny yearned to know. She knelt to smooth leaves and debris from the face of a large stone.

Fairer Than had attended Queer Youth. Though she hardly appeared to be a teen, young faerie did have a school to go to. Bunny knew whom to ask—

Or more accurately, what. She laid her palm against the rock's face and spoke:

Thou Rock,
whose home this is,
since the first Dawn and
the first Song of Bliss,
and from whom not one thing
escapes thy visage,
Tell me where the School of Daughters is.

The stone glowed. Letters formed on its surface, written in the Lost Language. The stone helpfully scrawled a pointing arrow for Bunny.

"Thank you!" Bunny said.

The stone's arrow, then fading, indicated a tangled growth. Bunny approached, knelt, and pushed aside foliage. Within lay a dark tunnel through the woven branches. Bunny set her hat firmly on her head, placed her broom before her, and then crawled forwards, pushing her broom ahead.

The tunnel wound and deepened, but Bunny was not long in her crawl before she heard a voice, traveling from within the forest.

"Oh, what a wondrous sight to behold!" the little male voice exclaimed. Bunny made her way to where light shimmered through the leaves. She came to a stop, sat back, and cautiously pulled aside a branch to see.

There, in a lush, moss-covered clearing, sunbeams shone through the canopy above. A frog in full coat and tails stood erect within one beam, his feet perched on a branch before four faerie daughters, each one bearing a black pot full of treasures. The frog raised his little arms in praise.

"Four pots of gold, all in a row!" he cried. "Very good, girls! And remember: forever should these be hidden, from the sight of mortal eyes that do seek them!" He then produced a large book—one large in relationship to himself—and donned spectacles. He flipped the ancient pages.

"Unless they be of hearts true and pure, deserving of such illumination! Etcetera, etcetera, page 7678th's and a half, rule 7687 of the coda of faeries. Ahem!" He shut the book. "And now let's move on to our next lesson: hiding the pot."

He gestured engagingly towards his students. "A task you will all most certainly pass! Nary a potential dropout among you." The girls giggled at his words.

He then looked askance towards the forest, his bespectacled gaze stern.

"Speaking of dropouts," he added coldly. Fairer Than stood in the shadows.

Bunny put a hand to her throat. Compared to the bright faerie maidens dutifully bearing their pots, Fairer Than seemed a lurking wolf among them.

The frog bounded for Fairer Than. "Well, well! If it isn't the faerie quite contrary!"

"Schoolmaster," Fairer Than greeted, her voice low and deliberate.

"Ahem!" The schoolmaster stood before her on the forest floor, hands on his hips. "And where is thy pot, wayward daughter?"

"My 'pot,' sir?"

The schoolmaster jumped up and down. "Thy pot! Pot! *Pot!*"

Fairer Than put a thoughtful finger to her chin. "Ah, that pot, sir." She stepped aside.

Behind her stood a great tree's trunk. Fairer Than raised two fingers, gesturing near her forehead. "As the schoolmaster wishes—" She swept the fingers across the tree. "So it is revealed." Behind her hand's sweeping passage, a hollow appeared in the tree trunk, bearing a black iron pot within.

"Ah, that's more like it!" The schoolmaster hopped up to the hole and peered. "Now let's see—"

As Bunny watched, a sprite came to hover by her eyes, its little gaze inquisitive.

"What's this?" the frog cried. His legs dangled over the

pot's edge as he scrutinized the contents. "Lollie Frankie vinyl records...ticket stubs to the celluloid pictures theater in Little Salem—'Young Witch' *magazine*?" He bounced out of the hollow and landed on Fairer Than's chest. "And *where* is thy gold, young lady?"

"Spent, sir," Fairer Than said with an innocent gaze. "Faerie gold does not go far, these days."

The schoolmaster grabbed her by the earlobe and leapt, pulling her along. "Come here!"

"Ow," Fairer Than said.

He landed on her bosom again as they stood before the other girls, and raised an imperious finger. "Now look at them! So many springs thy junior and already the promising blossoms of the Court!"

Fairer Than did look, her gaze sliding to where the girls stood. One faerie whispered behind her hand to another and they giggled.

"What hast thou to show for thyself and thy wasted years—" A twig appeared in the frog's hand and he leapt up, swatting Fairer Than. She bowed out of the way. "*Traipsing* about in the outside world, plying thy sword and wiles to *wastrel* adventuring and so-called legend-making? So how was that Bill Shakespeare, eh?"

Bunny fed the sprites biscuit crumbs as she listened to the schoolmaster's tantrum.

"Think thou can return, taking up proper courtly airs, looking as thou dost?" he yelled, again standing before Fairer Than while perched on her bosom. He smacked a red lock of hair out of the way as Fairer Than looked over at the other faeries. "Explain thy hair! The rumpled state of thy dishabille!"

"I lead a rambunctious life," Fairer Than said, grinning at the girls.

"This I say to your rambunctiousness, Fairer Than!" the

schoolmaster cried. He leapt away for the hollow in the tree.

The sounds of magazines tearing and of records smashing ensued. Fairer Than looked on, surprised, as torn pages fluttered to the ground.

Oh dear. Bunny's heart hurt at the sight. Finally, the schoolmaster's rampage ceased. He bounded away from the hollow and hopped along the clearing. The faerie maidens turned and followed, chins raised and pots in hand.

"Now ladies," the frog announced, "if you'll follow me, we will continue with our lesson of 'hiding the pot'."

As one row, they exited the clearing.

Fairer Than reached into her pot and pulled out a broken record, seemingly contemplating its damaged state. Bunny pushed the branches aside of her hiding place.

She emerged into the sunlit clearing with her broom in hand, Fairer Than turning to look at her.

CHAPTER FIVE

"Bunny," Fairer Than said, and her tone was warm.

"Oh, Fairer Than, your records." When Bunny neared, she touched the one Fairer Than held and inspected the damage. The 45 single was of a Lollie Frankie song: *Where the Girls Are*. "I can try a spell to make them whole again, but they'll never sound the same."

Fairer Than smiled and put the broken record back into her pot. "Don't worry, Bunny. I haven't the means to play them, anyway."

"You don't have a record player?"

Fairer Than waved her hand before the hollow, sealing it again. "Where in these woods would I be able to plug it in?"

"Good point." Bunny smiled.

"It's good to see you, Bunny." Fairer Than turned to her, standing close.

Bunny stepped back, her broom in both hands. "Yes. Well, Fairer Than." She took a breath, then brought a finger up. "I came to see you because I think you enchanted me, Fairer Than, and I want you to lift that enchantment, right now."

"Enchantment, Bunny?"

"Yes! An enchantment of me! Ever since I've met you, I've been—well, I want it to stop, right now."

Fairer Than's brow lifted. "I've cast no spell, Bunny."

"Fairer Than," Bunny said patiently.

"It's true." Fairer Than grinned, and Bunny stared at her generous-lipped mouth. "Unlike my sisters, I care not for magicks. I like to rely on my...physical merits, alone."

Bunny huffed. "Don't tell me this is what you *really* look like."

"Oh, it is." Fairer Than stepped closer. "Would you like to find out?"

Bunny turned, ready to jump on her broomstick.

"Wait," Fairer Than bade behind her. When Bunny looked, Fairer Than had raised a solemn hand—not to stop her, but in a gesture as one made when pledging. A butterfly fluttered, and sunlight fell on Fairer Than as she spoke.

"I swear upon great grandfather's teeth and tail, I did not enchant you, Bunny." Fairer Than reached into her bosom and drew out a breast dagger. "Would you like that in blood?"

"No! Put that away!" Bunny ran forwards as Fairer Than positioned the dagger's point against her forearm.

Fairer Than did as Bunny asked, the dagger tucked back inside her bodice front. Bunny raised a hand to her forehead and sighed.

"I believe you, Fairer Than. I'm sorry to have bothered you." She turned away again to leave.

"How did you know to come here, Bunny?" Fairer Than asked behind her, curious. Bunny paused. "The school is only known to faeries, as is its whereabouts. Those mortals who seek out the faerie kind, the forest would mislead..."

Bunny smiled despite herself, her hands on her broom.

She remembered another time and another clearing, filled with sunbeams.

"To forever wander the forest floor, lost," Fairer Than continued. She approached, her step soft on the moss. "Until they decide it best to return to their homes. You are not one of those mortals."

Fairer Than neared, and Bunny felt again the heat of her physical presence.

"The forest likes you," Fairer Than said, low. A female sprite hovered close, her wings like a butterfly. Or perhaps she had been the butterfly in the clearing, all along. Bunny raised a finger for her to land on. The sprite touched her toes down lightly.

"Do you come to the forest often, Bunny?" Fairer Than asked softly, her voice at Bunny's shoulder.

"No." The sprite glided around Bunny. "No. Not anymore." She remembered and related the memory...

In the clearing, faerie women danced.

Bunny was a small child again, looking up at the faeries she'd discovered. The frog schoolmaster played merrily on a fiddle while a grasshopper strummed his mandolin. A sprite blew powerfully on his flower trumpet. The women circled, diaphanous gowns fluttering, and petals wafted in their wake, fallen from their flower crowns. Sprites flew off with Bunny's little witch's hat, and a faerie paused in her dancing, looked down, and smiled.

She knelt and crowned Bunny with flowers. Bunny stared up at a woman in sunlight and falling petals, and felt her world glow.

Bunny returned from memory and ceased telling the story, her broomstick resting against her shoulder. The sprite did a handstand on Bunny's finger.

"When my aunties found out where I'd been, they flipped!" Bunny finally murmured, smiling. "They said

I could have been faerie-abducted. I'd not been back since…not until now."

"Your aunties were correct." Bunny glanced over at Fairer Than, who stood away, intent on the flower crown she weaved. The sprite pushed Bunny's broom from her grasp, causing it to fall.

"Hey," Bunny softly said, but the same sprite zoomed back, catching Bunny's brim. She removed Bunny's hat.

"The faerie kind are fond of mortal children, and you must have been a beautiful child." Fairer Than approached, connecting the ends of her flower crown. She laid the crown gently on Bunny's head. "I would have remembered you."

Bunny became lost in a green-eyed gaze, a sensual and resinous scent on hot skin, and felt Fairer Than's warm hand caress her cheek. "Is that when you fell in love with the faerie, Bunny? Is that why you are here now…with me?"

"Fairer Than." Bunny moved Fairer Than's hand away, and their palms touched. "I have a girlfriend. Her name is…"

"Yes?" Fairer Than's eyes lit, a fiery conflagration behind the green of her irises.

"Her name…"

"Yes…" Fairer Than drew nearer.

"It's De-De-De—*beat it! Dematerialize!*" Bunny struck her own head with her wand.

Fairer Than disappeared from sight as magic sparkled. Then Bunny saw blue sky and treetops. She inhaled fresh air, blowing across the lake's surface. She dropped like a stone and hit the water.

Cold! If anything could drive Fairer Than's heat and mesmerizing beauty from Bunny's mind, the shock of lake water would. Enveloped, Bunny kicked up and then broke surface, gulping for air.

"*Dean*," she gasped. "Her name is Dean—"

Bunny tread water and floated, the waves and wind her only companions.

"That's telling her, Bunny," she muttered. She kicked and set off for shore.

By the time she'd reached shallow water, Bunny was resolved: she needn't see Fairer Than, ever again. Fairer Than was a dark faerie, unmistakably, and her personal allure was indeed, powerful. But Bunny had met plenty of powerful creatures and humans with extra powers. A dark faerie needed handling in the usual manner—with avoidance. Bunny grumbled and hauled herself up a rising bank.

"No enchantment involved? Fine! I can forget your beautiful eyes." She plopped down, exhausted. When she reached up to wring her hair, her fingers encountered the drooping petals from her crown of flowers. Her fingers stilled.

"Really looks like that, my pointy hat," she muttered.

"Hello, Bunny," a woman's voice murmured.

"Hello," another greeted.

Bunny glanced at the water, surprised. Longhaired women swam, their tresses trailing. More broke the surface with only their heads showing and looked at her. They all wore the same benign and inquisitive expression.

"Hello Daughters of the Water," Bunny greeted in return. Unlike the faeries of the forest, Bunny liked seeking out the faeries of the lake and spending time with them. They never threatened to drown anyone, unlike some of their kin (such as the mermaids) and tended towards cool, calm conversations. Bunny had never known them to be very mischievous or even playful, and if others found them boring in their predictability, she didn't.

"Met our dark sister?" one inquired.

"Met her?" Bunny grinned, hands on her hips. "If all your sisters of the fire are like her, mortal kind is doomed to enslavement."

"That one? A faerie of fire?" one said.

"Oh no, Bunny," another said.

"No."

"No."

Bunny's smile faded at the small chorus of *no's* from the swimming women.

"But I saw her light a cigarette, by will alone," she said.

"Aye, for she is of another kind, entirely," one softly responded. She rose slightly out of the water, her hair covering her body. "Part of Mother, part of Father…"

"Part of flesh, part of fire…" spoke another, gliding.

"Irresistible e'en to faerie," the first added, smiling up at Bunny.

"Indeed," a third muttered.

Bunny looked from one to the other.

"Beware, Bunny," came the soft warning as the women sank beneath the water.

"Beware."

CHAPTER SIX

"The water faeries said that?" Blanchet exclaimed.

"Yes!"

Bunny was back home in her room at Baker Cottage, dressing. Night was falling, and she'd already finished feeding the hens and watering the garden. Aunt Agoosta was in the kitchen, starting the dinner stew in the kitchen caldron. But Bunny planned to eat later; she was going out with Dean that night.

Blanchet's visage floated in the mist showing in Bunny's vanity mirror while Bunny wiggled into a slip. She'd already donned her girdle and stockings. Scrying via a reflective surface—whether a mirror, crystal ball, or a bowl of water—was the usual way to remote-communicate in Little Salem, and Blanchet had adapted easily. However, Bunny did have conventional phone service thanks to vampires being unable to cast a reflection.

"So if Fairer Than isn't a faerie of fire, what is she?" Blanchet said.

"Well, what do you think the four parts mean?" Bunny retrieved her dress, laid on the patchwork quilt of her bed.

"Hm." Blanchet looked down, her arm moving as if drawing. "'Mother' is for Mama Earth. 'Father' for Papa Sky. Flesh is for us mortals." She then held up her notebook for Bunny to see. She'd drawn a planet with a female face, a male face with stars, and two afro-haired mortals. She brought the notebook down again. "And fire is…" Blanchet's eyes widened.

"Dang, girl, *what* have you gotten yourself into?" she said.

"*Nothing*, Blanchet." Bunny finished pulling her dress down over her head and wiggled more, adjusting the fit. She then reached behind for the zipper.

"Truth, Bunny." Blanchet grinned. "Now that you know it isn't enchantment…what is it?"

Bunny snorted. "Gorgeous faerie looks and me going ga-ga over them." After zipping, she buttoned on her three-quarter sleeved sweater with the tiny embroidered flowers at the collar.

"And?" Blanchet enticed.

"Blanchet." Bunny looked at her. "That's all. And I'll tell you how I know."

"How?"

Bunny placed her witch's hat on her head and grinned. "Because Fairer Than doesn't make my heart go *rum-rum-ritty* like Dean can."

"Really?"

"Really."

"If thinking of Dean puts a look like that on your face, I'm convinced." Blanchet brought up a candlesnuffer and began capping the candle flames before her own mirror. "Have fun tonight!"

"Thanks! Night, Blanchet." Bunny wet her fingers and

quickly pinched her own candles out. When she descended for below, she thought of Dean and smiled.

Hello, Bunny, Fairer Than said in Bunny's head.

Bunny stumbled and fell into the living room. She landed on her behind.

"*Oi!* What's that racket?" Agoosta called from the kitchen.

"I-I'm okay!" Bunny called. She struggled to get up.

"Ye *bad child*, Bunny!" Aunt Weirdie suddenly cried, appearing seemingly from nowhere. Bunny shrieked at her aunt's sudden appearance and received a hard poke from her aunt's gnarled finger. Wizened and tiny, Weirdette stared indignantly with bulbous eyes, her straw-like, black hair sticking out from beneath her crumpled witch's hat.

"Wha—what did I do?" Bunny exclaimed.

"Ye think ye'll be takin' yer pretty self out, now?" Weirdette loudly mocked. Bunny stared down at her aunt, baffled.

"Yes! I finished my chores and my homework. You all promised!"

"Ha! Listen to the bad witch!" Aunt Hauntie hobbled in from the sitting room, her peg leg clacking on the wooden floor. She eyed Bunny with her permanent squint, her cob pipe sticking up from her mouth. Her warty chin jutted. "Think ye can sneak orf from school and us li'l old ladies not know, eh, you ungrateful child?"

"Bad-bad," Weirdette tutted.

"How—?" Bunny then hurried to look in the kitchen. A little, red demon sat at the kitchen table, enjoying brie and bread, just as Bunny had expected.

"*Pippita!*" Bunny accused.

"Hiya, Bunny," Pippita greeted while Agoosta worked before the kitchen hearth. "This is the best brie you've made yet! How'd that truancy work out for ya?"

Weirdette poked Bunny in the ribs. Bunny turned.

"So! Ye think ye can do without a day of education, eh?" Weirdette said.

"Think ye know all the spells, all the potions, all the lore—" Hauntette chastised.

"Okay," Bunny yelled. "I shouldn't have cut school. I'm sorry. But I'm still a very good witch!"

Her aunts stared.

"Ooooo," they exclaimed in unison. They jumped her.

"No hat!"

"No wand!"

"No broom!"

Before Bunny could blink, her aunts had divested her of her hat and wand and shoved her out the front door.

"Lessee how ya fair in them formidable woods *now*, ya *very* goodie witch!" The door slammed behind Bunny.

"Have a nice night, dearie!" Hauntette called from within the house. The aunts cackled in glee.

Bunny looked fearfully out into the darkness, beyond the front garden's gate into the Enchanting Forest. Leaves softly rustled in the wind, and behind them, tiny eyes gleamed.

～

Beneath a full moon, hot rods roared in Forever Remember Cemetery, spitting flames from their tail pipes. Drivers triggered their hellfire injection systems and sent their rods careening for the sky. But most stood parked, showing off paint jobs and custom interiors. Dean strutted among them in a white tee and dungarees, a toothpick between her teeth.

The rumble of cars and the presence of girls—while she

waited for one girl in particular—was perfection.

"Can't get better than this," Dean said.

"Hey Dean," a skull girl in cat eye frames said.

"Hey Dean," greeted the winged devil girl lounging beside skull girl.

"'Ey," Dean said with a grin, and strolled on. A warthog demon with tusks and wearing a leather jacket looked over. With him stood two smaller demons, one with a greasy pompadour.

"Ayyy Dean," the large demon drawled. "Ya seen that cute, blonde witch around? I wanna say 'hi'." His large belly shook and his buddies guffawed. "She oughta go out with a *real* demon sometime. And not some…biter," he added.

"Hoo, bud," the demon with the pompadour said.

Dean rushed up and socked the big demon hard on his massive chin. She kept pounding until he went down, too stunned to retaliate.

"Yeah, Dean," a ghoul girl called cautiously. The littler demons watched the one-sided fight, wide-eyed. "Here comes yer girl."

Dean rose quickly, looking for Bunny. Warthog lay insensate.

Dean swiveled on her heel and pointed at Warthog.

"Thanks for the fight," she said, and winked. She ran for Bunny.

⁓

Bunny cautiously entered the cemetery with a tied bunch of basil atop her head. After a nervous walk through the woods, she'd reached the noisy company of people at last. But even with kids around and cars roaring overhead, she didn't feel ready to let her guard down. The greater faeries, like Fairer Than, did not concern themselves with mortals overly much, but their tinier kin, mischievous and bored, liked to cause trouble. Especially for those mortals who had come to their attention.

Bunny looked warily about, spying no little folk. Being kicked out of the house with no wand and hat made her aunts' lesson clear: she had yet to learn independence from magical tools.

"Hey Bunny," Dean said, running up to her.

"Dean!" Bunny cried, and flung herself into Dean's arms. She kissed her.

"Wow, what a greeting," Dean said happily when they'd parted. She put an arm around Bunny, and they walked up the cemetery hill path, away from parked hot rods. "Is that a new hat?"

"No," Bunny laughed. She removed the herb bundle. "A bunch of basil helps ward off the wee folk. My aunties shoved me out the door without my wand, hat, *and* broom."

"Wow. Tough lesson. What'd you do, step on faerie mushrooms?"

Bunny laughed again and embraced Dean more. Dean was a cool-bodied presence; she had no breath or heat. But passion would light her face for simple things like engines or a good brawl, and that drew Bunny into Dean's earnestness and happiness.

They took a seat on a sealed coffin left above ground and looked down the hill. Batboys had run off with a Jack O'Lantern's head and were rolling it as fast as they could from his pursuing body.

"Oh, tonight's nice," Bunny sighed. "Look at all the creatures, ghouls, and undead…"

"We always hang out with the creatures, ghouls, and undead," Dean remarked.

"Well, tonight it's especially nice."

Dean looked at her, then kissed her on the side of the head. "Everything okay, Bunny?"

"Wha—why do you ask?"

"Pip' said you lit out from school, today. Doesn't sound like you."

"I had something to do." The last thing Bunny wanted to think about was Fairer Than. She turned to Dean.

"Can I tell you about it later?" she asked softly. "I don't feel like talking about it now."

"Sure."

"Really?"

"Yeah. I've got all the time in the Twilight World to be with my girl," Dean grinned.

A smile lit Bunny's face. She put her arms around Dean's neck and moved close for a kiss.

BONK

The impact to the back of her head sent her forehead smacking into Dean's.

"Ow!" Bunny held her head, angered, and looked quickly around. Tiny sprites winged away. Dean picked up a pinecone: the missile thrown.

A hot rod roared above, spewing hellfire, and thick tentacles waved from the windows. Dean tossed the pinecone.

"Let's go flying!" Dean grabbed Bunny's hand.

"But—I don't have my broom," Bunny said, still disorientated by the pinecone blow.

"That's okay, Bunny. You got me." Dean grinned and ran with Bunny up the hill. Bunny's smile returned, and she forgot all about malicious little faeries.

When they reached the top, Dean urged Bunny to climb on to her back. With Bunny holding tight, Dean ran and leapt off, gliding for the big face of the moon.

⤳

"Oh, that was great!" Bunny enthused. Dean cradled Bunny in her arms and carried her along the path back to Baker cottage. In the distant night sky, the hot rod with flailing tentacles still flew, skywriting flaming patterns. Bunny hugged Dean's neck.

"Feel better?" Dean said.

Bunny's heart filled. "Thank you."

Pap

Something hit Dean's chest and fell into Bunny's lap. They looked down. Garlic.

"Oh nn—ga-ga-ga-*garlic*!" Dean sneezed, thunderous.

Bunny fell out of Dean's arms and on to the forest floor as Dean transformed with a loud *poof*, her garlic allergy activating her bat form. Dean flapped miserably in the air and sneezed again.

"Oh, Dean!" Bunny quickly turned from where she lay at the sound of old ladies cackling. Weirdette and Hauntette stood behind the garden's low front gate, its wooden doors firmly shut. Hauntette brandished a slingshot.

"Oi, we got the vampire good!" The two giggled again. Agoosta called from within.

"Girls," she hollered. "'Worst Dressed of the Vampire Ball' is on the telly!" The two aunts turned as one and scurried for the door.

"Dean, go ahead home! I'll be okay!" Bunny called up to her suffering girlfriend. Dean flew up and away, sneezing.

"S-see ya!" Dean bade, flying out into the night, and then she was gone.

Bunny sighed and hugged herself, holding on to the good feelings of their date. Once the hug was done, she picked up a broken mushroom that lay beside her, the purple cap dotted with white spots.

"You, Dean, are too amazing," she murmured.

Then she noticed the mushroom's state.

Bunny attempted to get up.

"*Broke our faerie ring!*" a sprite screamed, and flew at her. More pulled on Bunny's hair and clothes.

"Broke our ring!"

"*Horrid* mortal!"

"Wait!" Bunny cried. "Ow!"

"Shoo." A hand came down and waved the little faeries away. Fairer Than knelt beside Bunny.

"Broke our dancing circle, she did!" a flying sprite cried, and shook his fist.

"You've another o'er the glen," Fairer Than said, stern. "Begone; I give my protection to Bunny, the good witch." She scooped Bunny up in her arms. The sprites fled.

Bunny felt herself lifted as if she were no more than a feather. Fairer Than exuded strength and heat. She was a furnace, a mini-sun.

"H-how are you doing this?" Bunny said. "Carrying me?"

"Do I appear so frail?" Fairer Than's tone was light as she walked slowly down the path for Bunny's home. Her hips swayed, and the motion rocked Bunny in her arms.

"No, you're..." *Bigger, taller, stronger, more beautiful than any faerie I've seen.* "You're surprising."

"I was born far stronger than faerie, Bunny."

"What are you, Fairer Than?" Bunny whispered. Fairer Than seated Bunny on the front gate's stone post.

"There you are, Bunny, safe and sound." Fairer Than looked at her indulgently.

"What are you?" Bunny repeated.

"I would see you to your front door, but your aunties have hung a horseshoe above it, and I am allergic to horseshoes," Fairer Than said. Bunny stared into her eyes.

"Fairer Than, what are you," she asked.

Fire flickered behind Fairer Than's irises.

"Thrice thou have asked," she said softly. "The answer, thou shall have. I am as flesh as you, Bunny. I am half-part faerie…one-part mortal."

She leaned close.

"And one-part…"

Her mouth neared.

"Dragon," she whispered against Bunny's lips.

Bunny's head turned.

"*By this Devil's Hat, I am changed! A mouse! A mouse! A mouse!*" Bunny incanted and bit down on the mushroom still in her hand.

Bunny disappeared, her sweater, dress, and the rest of her clothing suddenly empty. They crumpled to the post's top. Bunny wiggled her tiny furry body out of the sweater's end and dropped to the garden floor. She scampered away through the bluebells and other flowering plants. Even as she worked all four mouse paws and her tail—grateful for her lessons in learning the movement of animals—she felt Fairer Than's gaze follow her.

Bunny gained the rosemary bush by the front door. Once hidden behind it, she stood up on her haunches and dared to look back. A poem came to her, a song sung long ago.

OH DRAGON,
Mightiest of Creation.
The Stars are your sail ways,
the Universe, your kingdom!
Great Dragon,
thou art our progenitors,
our Masters, and among

> Mortal kind,
> our seducers.

Fairer Than rested hands on the shut front gate, the faint aura of a winged dragon rising behind her.

Bunny squeaked.

CHAPTER SEVEN

"WHEN the world began, Dragon was right there, breathin' stars and suns, beatin' broad wings 'pon the black of the universe and laughin' fire with the first of the gods.

"They embodied the light and the dark; the fury cosmic and the serenity divine. 'Neath one wing lay hope, and 'neath the other, damnation.

"To gaze 'pon their frightening beauty was to be both blessed and cursed."

At Pippita's words, a vision came to Bunny, but it was not of Fairer Than. In her mind's eye she saw a lone woman, caught outside while those of her mountainside village hid, gazing up at a massive dragon's body passing slowly above her.

"So it only stood to reason that when dragons walked the Earth, they should become the most powerful, most wealthy, and most omnipotent pontiffs o'er mortal kind!"

A boy king, alone on his dragon throne, sitting in a hall piled with treasures and gold, Bunny thought.

"And if a mortal had even a drop o' their blood, the shine o' the fire heart was in that one's countenance and bearing, for that one was the descendant of a dawn of sun births."

Bunny's eyes closed. She saw one like Fairer Than, dark-haired and noble, carrying bow and arrows. At her belt hung teeth, and her tribe bowed before her.

"They were *dragon*, man, and their passion and ardor produced fruitful bounty like apples in Eden. If a dragon so much as breathed on a woman, she'd find herself ripe with *ten* babies!"

"Pippita!" Bunny's eyes opened and she laughed. The sounds of the school cafeteria came to the fore, and visions of dragon kin faded from her mind's eye. Blanchet sat beside her with a hand to her cheek, enrapt by Pippita's tale. They were dawdling at school's end, wanting to hear Pippita's rendition of dragon lore.

"It's true!" Pippita exclaimed, throwing her short arms out in emphasis. "So how much heavy breathin' have Fairer Than, the part-dragon, and *you* been doin', Bunny?"

Bunny's humor dissipated and she glared. The apple she'd picked up as a snack remained untouched. She touched it briefly with her wand.

Voice begone, she instructed the apple, and the spell sank into its red skin.

"Fairer Than can't get Bunny pregnant, Pippita," Blanchet dismissed.

"What kinda future witch doctor are you?" Pippita said. She grabbed Bunny's apple. "It doesn't matter with dragons because—" Pippita tossed the apple into her wide mouth and gulped it. "They can shape-change! Time to check if there's a bun in your oven, Bunny!"

Bunny coolly ignored her and finished her milk. She put the carton down. "Well, that explains why she has such an effect on me. I can't get her out of my mind."

"To exist as a dragon is like being an embodiment of the elemental powers themselves," Blanchet said to her in a hushed voice. "Extraordinary."

"Dragons are also living magic, like the faerie and the unicorns," Bunny added, solemn.

"Yeah, just being in their presence is enchantment," Pippita said. "And—"

Pippita clutched her throat, wide-eyed. What emitted next was only a wheeze.

Bunny rose from the cafeteria table with her books and departed. Blanchet glanced quizzically at Pippita and her sudden muteness, and then followed, donning her backpack.

"But aren't dragons more than what faeries and unicorns seem to be?" Blanchet argued by Bunny's side. "Aren't they somehow akin to gods themselves?"

"So the lore may say," Bunny said. Pippita caught up with them and hopped up and down, pointing to her throat.

"Dang, girl, maybe you should marry Fairer Than." Blanchet laughed.

"Tsk, Blanchet. You forget; Fairer Than is part-faerie, and faeries don't have real hearts." Bunny looked back in irritation at Pippita, who tugged desperately on Bunny's pencil skirt.

"That's for snitching on me to my aunties, Pippita!" Bunny said hotly. Pippita flipped her the bird, then two birds, and stalked off.

Blanchet scoffed. "The faeries not having real hearts?" They exited the school and walked down the front steps. "That never bothered you before, Bunny."

"Well, it didn't bother me like it didn't bother you when you crushed on a zombie boy, until that boy wanted to eat your brain," Bunny teased.

"You got me," Blanchet admitted. She stood aside while Bunny prepared her parked broom for their ride home. A wolf boy and monster boy in letter jackets had made off with a skeleton guy's skull, and after a game of toss, lounged on the school's steps while the skull sputtered. Bunny levitated her broom and strapped her books to the back rack. She looked over to where Scott argued with his girlfriend, Madeline, via a borrowed crystal ball, the witch girl owner patiently waiting. Bunny recalled Pippita mentioning the two possibly breaking up; they'd been fighting since Fairer Than's appearance at Shivers.

Well, Madeline had always been insecure about her snake hair, Bunny thought. She suspected that Fairer Than's red locks had instilled more than jealousy.

Madeline abruptly cut the scrying connection, leaving her boyfriend frustrated.

"Madeline didn't like it that Scott looked at Fairer Than," Blanchet mused, having noticed the altercation too. "Fairer Than's beauty alone is pretty much wrecking them—and the irony? I doubt Fairer Than even knows who they are and that it's even happening."

"That's dragon power for you," Bunny said. She hopped sidesaddle on to her broomstick, steadying it. Blanchet seated herself sideways behind Bunny, balancing as a passenger would on a bike or motorcycle. She held Bunny firmly around the waist and her top hat to her afro. Bunny urged her broom back, and then took off for the sky.

"I've heard that dragons have hearts," Blanchet stated loudly when they sped by Little Salem's clock tower in the town square. "I wonder where they keep them?"

"In a chest, that's in a goose egg, under a goose, in a room, inside a castle, in the middle of a lake?" Bunny yelled above the sound of wind. A flying hot rod appeared and kept pace with them. It popped a wheelie, spewing flames.

"Ayyyy, sweeties!"

"Heyyy hotties! C'mon, baby!"

Bunny veered away from the catcalling demons and pointed her broom for Blanchet's home.

After a ten-minute flight, Bunny slowed her broom and descended into a neighborhood of elegant, old buildings with wrought iron balconies. Weeping willows rustled, hung with Spanish moss, and the smell of gumbo and frying catfish wafted. Two small children ran squealing before a lumbering zombie.

"Fairer Than's part-mortal," Blanchet remarked as Bunny glided for the street. "Dragon heart, part-mortal…"

"Now stop," Bunny admonished. She brought the broom to a halt, still levitating. "I love Dean. I'm not interested in Fairer Than."

"That's not what you said at school." Blanchet hopped off and stood before her. She looked at Bunny. "'I can't get her out of my mind,' you said."

Bunny adjusted her balance to return Blanchet's gaze. "That's dragon magic talking, Blanchet."

"Maybe. But I think you know as well as I do; the best magic happens when there's a connection."

Bunny bit her lip.

"Kinda makes you want to check it out, doesn't it?" Blanchet added softly.

Bunny didn't answer. She only nodded in farewell and turned back to her broomstick. She headed for the sky.

As she crossed above Little Salem, she thought about Blanchet's suggestion. Surely she didn't mean that Bunny step out on Dean?

I'm not that kind of girl.

And the idea of breaking up with Dean in order to pursue Fairer Than made her feel like she'd hacked a limb off. Such pain inspired an odd sense of relief.

"It really is dragon magic," she decided.

≈

Bunny alighted at home, and once upstairs in her bedroom, her princess phone rang on her nightstand.

"Dean?" she answered after jumping on to her bed and picking up the receiver. She lay stomach-down on the quilt's surface.

"'Ey babe! How'd you know it was me?"

"Because you're a vampire, silly. Only you would call me on the phone." Bunny grinned and looked at the picture frame on the nightstand. The name *DEAN* was handwritten in it.

"Yeah, well, I wish I could use a magic mirror, because I miss seeing my girl's face, every minute of the day!"

Bunny giggled. A pneumatic impact wrench worked loudly in the background. Dean was at Soupy's Gas again, working on her gang's hot rod. Bunny imagined Dean in her mechanic's coveralls.

"Sorry I couldn't pick you up after school today, Bunny. The guys really needed me at the garage."

"It's okay, Dean."

"But there's a dance coming up! It's this Friday. I just saw the flyer. Queer Youth is hosting it. Wanna go?"

"Oh, Dean, you know I do!"

"Cool! Love you, Bunny!"

"Love you, Dean!"

Bunny hung up, patted her worn, stuffed rabbit toy that sat on her bed, and went to her closet. She looked through her outfits and picked out one for the dance, a dress with scoop collar and bow. She briefly danced the Bop with it.

Her phone rang again.

"Dean?" Bunny answered.

"Hello, Bunny."

Bunny's heart jumped to her throat. As a voice alone, the self-confident tone was unmistakable.

"Fairer Than?" Bunny said, swallowing.

"How sweet. You remember my voice." Fairer Than's low tone lightened, as if she grinned.

"How…where are you calling from?"

"Goodie Gertie's. I'd asked for her scrying ball, but she hasn't one."

"That's because her face broke her last four." Bunny did not mean that as an insult. Poor Gertie was considered the most hideous-looking witch in Little Salem. However, Gertie was still a little old lady, and apparently dealing with a dragon-faerie darkening her doorstep. Bunny wondered if she should hurry over. "What are you doing at Goodie Gertie's?" she demanded.

"Clearing her back field."

"That field has *huge* boulders and several dead trees on it!"

"Not anymore."

Fairer Than grinned, laid on her side and propped up on an elbow as she enjoyed a respite on Gertie's back porch. She idly held Gertie's candlestick phone and its mouthpiece near while her other elbow rested on her curving hip. The hand belonging to that elbow pressed the receiver to her ear. Her hands were roughened and soiled from her labor, and she knew her face and kirtle had their smudges as well. But Fairer Than felt sufficiently invigorated, and, therefore, in the mood for girl-chatting. Farther down the long length of her body, Mugg sat, perched atop her calf, and viewed the cleared field. Gertie looked on as well, with her black cat draped over her hunch. She cackled.

Fairer Than had uprooted all dead trees and tossed them and the giant boulders into a pile. To extend her fun, she planned to make kindling of the trees, later. She sniffed herself, believing her faerie scent bore a touch of dragon pungency. Would Bunny—like the women of yore—find such sweaty vigor attractive?

"Did Gertie have a contract with you?" Bunny asked, and her voice held accusation.

"Oh, nothing like that, Bunny," Fairer Than reassured.

"Really?"

"You sound surprised." Fairer Than glanced at the mouthpiece, thinking it a shame she couldn't smell Bunny as well. The young witch favored a pleasing l'eau de toilette: Damascene rose and jasmine. Fairer Than knew her Damascene roses.

"The faerie don't do favors for free." Bunny's tone was cold.

"True. But unlike the Folk, my dragon-side likes to… flex itself at times." Fairer Than glanced over to Goodie Gertie, who still chuckled, her bulbous and bloodshot eye looking on approvingly. The old witch hobbled for her doorway and the kitchen within. There was no danger of Fairer Than following. Like any sensible witch, Gertie had a horseshoe nailed above her doorframe.

"Bunny, this phone contraption is a remarkable invention," Fairer Than then said. "You sound like you are right here. With me."

"Is there a reason you're calling, Fairer Than?"

"Why, yes." Fairer Than sat up and rested her elbows on her knees. Mugg flew up and hovered before her gaze. He gripped the flyer he'd shown her earlier. The flyer read:

Dance! Hosted by Q-Youth.

"Queer Youth is having a dance," Fairer Than said. "Would you like to go?"

"I am going, but with my girlfriend, Fairer Than."

"Right. The one with a name like a stutter. De-de-de-de—"

❧

"Dean! Her name is Dean!" Bunny said, angered. "I don't intend to go out with you, Fairer Than, so give it up!"

"Interesting." Fairer Than's low tone seemed intrigued.

"W-what?"

"You haven't said anything about *not* liking me."

Bunny stilled.

"Soup's on!" Gertie yelled in the background. A triangle sounded, the ringing jarring Bunny from her frozen state.

"Ah, Gertie beats on her dinner chime." Fairer Than's voice was pleased. "Goodie Gertie has made me a hearty stew as a reward for my services." Bunny heard Fairer Than's body shift, and Bunny recalled strong, hot arms holding her aloft.

"I love a good cook," Fairer Than said, her voice intimate. "I'll see you at the dance, Bunny."

Click

Bunny slammed down her receiver, incensed.

She put on her full-length gardening apron with the big pockets and left to do her chores.

"Arrogant—dragon!" Bunny muttered as she tossed feed to the chickens in the back garden. "I wonder if faeries even sweat." She sniffed the air despite herself, recalling Fairer Than's scent, and smelled only earth and greenery. She fetched the watering can.

"Bunny," someone hissed from the stonewall.

When she glanced up, Dean waved from the other side, bent low. She wore her mechanic's coveralls.

Bunny put the can down and ran to the garden's back gate. Once outside, she took Dean's hand and hurried with her into the forest.

"Aunt Hauntie will throw a ladle at you, Dean," Bunny admonished but she giggled.

"That's why I was being sneaky," Dean grinned. She brought them to a stop and kissed Bunny on the lips.

Dean smelled of grease and engine oil. Bunny didn't care if it got on her clothes. She held Dean closer.

The nearby brush suddenly agitated. A tusked, demonic warthog burst through, red-eyed, bristling, and loudly squealing.

"Ha! That guy!" Dean picked up Bunny and held her above her head. She ran.

"Alley-oop!" Dean cried and tossed Bunny up into a tree. As Bunny struggled to wrap her arms and legs around a branch, Dean disappeared over a forest ridge, the warthog on her heels.

Bunny pulled her wand from her apron front. Dean returned through the foliage, the warthog galloping behind her. They ran by Bunny's tree with super-speed before she could cast a spell.

"Oh—come again, Dean!" Bunny called. She twirled her wand at the forest floor. A small orb of light formed, softball-sized. It floated, a fragile spell. Dean ran back with the warthog squealing madly.

"Jump!" Bunny yelled.

Dean leapt.

She rose in the air like one dunking a basketball, but

her hand put fingers to her lips instead, which she kissed. She then touched Bunny's lips. Below, the spell-orb burst as the warthog ran into it, but Bunny paid it no mind. She touched her own mouth and laughed as Dean fell and landed below.

"Ow! Give it up already," Dean chuckled. She shook a tusked pug off her trouser's leg, its hair bristly. She held out her arms for Bunny.

Once Bunny dropped into Dean's arms and regained her feet, the warthog pug yowled. Bunny tutted and picked him up, and he instantly stilled. Dean cautioned her not to cuddle him.

"This guy was a real ass at the cemetery car rally," Dean grumbled. "I gotta get back. He can hang out at the garage until the spell wears off." She held out her hands. Once she secured the pug beneath an arm, she took Bunny's hand.

"Remember when you turned a warlock into a frog for me?" Dean said as they walked back to the cottage. She was referring to the night they had first met; Spooky's cemetery fest. Warlock boys had attacked Dean's vampire gang, incensed by Dean having flirted with Bunny. The skeleton cops came to bust the fight and Bunny had fled with Dean into the forest—into the night. They'd escaped together.

That night, Bunny had chosen Dean.

"We make a great team, don't you think?" Dean said.

"We do." Bunny softly agreed, and felt the affirmation fit like a lost jigsaw puzzle piece.

She was still smiling when Dean left her in the back garden and ran back to Soupy's Gas, the warthog pug beneath her arm. Bunny returned to her chores. Hens fed, front and back garden watered and weeded, she swept the cottage's floor, then helped Aunt Agoosta with preparing dinner. After doing her homework, she ate dinner and joined her aunts in viewing a game show on TV. Once she returned to her room, she brought out old books borrowed from the witches' library. She intended to learn and practice internal magical skills until she could summon power without her wand's use.

When she finally closed her books, her aunts had long gone to bed. Inky, the black cat that chose to live with them, had already visited, left her a dead mouse, and departed for more nighttime hunting.

Bunny changed into a nightgown, and then snuggled under her bedcovers. She looked at the picture frame with Dean's name, remembering the night they escaped from the skeleton cops. She smiled.

Then she thought of Fairer Than.

She switched off her lamp, frustrated.

CHAPTER EIGHT

The following day proved uneventful, but at school's end Bunny found herself unaccountably tired as she waited before Shivers. She yawned mightily.

"HEY SLEEPY," Pippita shouted behind Bunny, activating her demonic visage. Her eyes bulged and her forked tongue undulated from her cavernous mouth. Bunny shrieked, wand in hand, but refrained from retaliating. Despite her pounding heart, she spun around and grinned. Pippita matched her indignant pose, hands on her hips.

"Found your voice, huh?" Bunny teased.

"Yeah, and no thanks to you, I discovered the antidote!" Pippita poked Bunny in the abdomen, her forked tongue lolling. "Cod liver oil. Funny, Bunny, ha-ha."

Bunny allowed herself to smirk.

Pippita then looked up at her, batting her eyelashes. "So...cheated on Dean yet?"

Bunny brought her wand down, magic exploding as sparkles. Once the sparkles dimmed, Pippita stood on the walk, a demonic red hen with horns, red eyes, and tail feathers as sharply pointed as her former tail.

Pippita squawked, feathers flying. Blanchet walked up, smiling. She looked at Pippita, then Bunny. As if decided she'd rather not ask, she headed inside the soda shop, Bunny following.

ȫ

"So she's calling you now?" They sat in a Shivers window booth, Bunny drinking milk while Blanchet regarded her, concerned. "I think you should tell Dean."

"I tried. Then things got complicated."

Blanchet frowned. "How do you mean?"

Bunny sighed. "This would have been easier if Fairer Than had simply been a faerie. A confrontation between Dean and her might result in Dean being turned into a frog or a slipper. That, I think I can handle. But with a dragon?" Bunny looked at Blanchet pointedly. "Especially when Dean *always* likes to fight first and never ask questions later?"

"Yikes." Blanchet's eyes widened. "You're right. Dragon versus vampire; that would *not* end well."

They watched Pippita, still a chicken, attempt to order a Flame soda at the counter.

"I'll take care of it," Bunny then assured, but the words came out as glum as she felt. "I just have to figure out how to get rid of a half-faerie, dragon, and part-mortal being who can't comprehend the word 'no.'" She glanced over as a bandaged hand waved near her. One of Dean's shop buddies, the diminutive and bandaged invisible boy, Burt, looked up at her in his dark glasses. He held up a folded note. On the front was written: *Bunny*.

Bunny accepted the note and read it as Burt waved hello to Blanchet, then walked away.

"Apples," Bunny said unhappily. "Dean's been held after school again. She had a fight with the werewolves."

Blanchet turned back after having watched Burt go, a smile of interest on her lips. "I think that's the second time this week Dean's missed meeting you here. For fighting, of course."

"Well, her gang and the werewolves are rivals." Bunny sat back and folded her arms. She knew she ought to be the supportive girlfriend, but she didn't care for the rivalry. She had nothing against the wolves; she'd grown up with most of them. She glanced at Blanchet, who was looking out the scenic window, humming. Since Burt was nowhere in sight on the walk, Bunny had to assume Blanchet was being mysterious about something else.

"What?" Bunny demanded.

"I still think you and Fairer Than would make a cute couple," Blanchet said.

"*Blanchet.*" Bunny laughed.

She flew Blanchet home thereafter. But her friend's playful statement nagged. She didn't want to entertain what if's.

Later that night, while helping Aunt Agoosta with preparing dinner, Bunny paused in appreciating the fragrant kale soup she cooked atop the stove. Placing the lid back on the pot, she set her spoon aside. She knew what would settle the question that had been plaguing her since the soda shop, once and for all.

"Aunt Agoosta…is it possible for a mortal to have a meaningful relationship with a part-mortal faerie?" Bunny pulled the tarts out of the oven as she asked the question. Agoosta looked over from the kitchen table where she rolled out dough. Agoosta was the youngest aunt in the house, and the heftiest. She was tall and broad with a face also having broadened with age. But she still curled the bangs of her hair and made up her eyelashes. She favored a bright red lipstick, which she used to paint herself cupid's bow lips. Agoosta looked at Bunny in surprise, her tiny and carefully plucked brows raised.

"Wot a question! I thought we taught ye that the creatures of the other-realms are a bad lot!" She resumed her rolling. "The faerie haven't souls or hearts to speak of. That's why they fool with ours. Out of *spite* and envy."

I know. You've said it so many times. Bunny recalled her child self, watching the faerie women dance. *Perhaps it's too late for me.*

"The devils, demons, and other monster kin," Agoosta continued as she rolled, "their existence is *defined* by mortal kin. Like it or not, we are linked to them. But the faeries have no need for the likes of us! Who's this part-faerie ye're thinking of now?"

Bunny finished racking the tarts for cooling. "There was a faerie who helped Goodie Gertie with her back field—"

"Oh!" Agoosta started, rolling pin in hand. Her lipsticked mouth made a little "o". "*That* one. Gertie did tell Hauntette about the faerie with the drop o' dragon in her! Goddess help any who has an interest in *that* one!"

Agoosta then chortled and brought out her dough cutter. "For once I'm thankful ye're involved with a *vampire*, Bunny."

Bunny nodded. She retrieved the fresh batch of tarts Agoosta had laid out on a second baking tray. She slid it into the oven.

Later that night, she studied more magic.

Fairer Than stood in the woods behind the Baker cottage and leaned her elbow against a tree, her other hand on her hip. At Goodie Gertie's insistence, Fairer Than had been moving boulders around on Gertie's property all day, until Gertie finally decided she had liked them where Fairer Than had first left them.

One loaf of bread and a pot of corn chowder later, Fairer Than walked into the lake to wash off the day's grime. She would have been to Bunny's home sooner if she hadn't dallied with the water daughters, swimming after them and catching their toes. Where other faerie brethren often shunned her, the water daughters remained curious, and Fairer Than appreciated that they never seemed to fear her. They always maintained an equilibrium as cool and smooth as their domain, and if they felt passion or even anger, it was only a level or two above that calm. Water, no matter how or when it was disturbed, always returned to that calm.

Thus, Fairer Than coaxed the water women into playing, as it gave her a chance to engage in their guileless simplicity, especially in contrast to the more capricious and willful mermaids.

After a while of chasing water maidens around the lake, Fairer Than emerged and with a small burst of internal dragon's heat, dried herself. She arrived at the cottage just as Bunny was changing to go to bed. Fairer Than watched Bunny through her upper story window, the bedroom shutters still open, and straightened. She looked past the garden's low stonewall and at the plants within.

A witch's garden was a line of defense in addition to the iron horseshoes nailed over doorways. The Baker's back garden was liberally planted with bluebells. Once a trespassing faerie brushed the blossoms, the bluebells would ring. However, Fairer Than had her own method for by-passing them.

While Bunny stretched and yawned, clad in her night-gown, Fairer Than hitched up the fabrics of her skirt and tucked them into her girdle. Legs free, she then ran for the garden's low stonewall.

She leapt, pushing her toes off the wall as she did so. She soared over the garden for the house.

CRACK

Fairer Than held on to Bunny's sill while her toes gripped the timber frame of the upper story. The force of her impact into the house produced a sizable crack in the Baker cottage's wall.

Bunny swiveled from her vanity at the sound, her boar's bristle hairbrush in hand.

"Hello, Bunny," Fairer Than greeted, and attempted nonchalance as she rested elbows on the sill.

Bunny shrieked. She ran for her bed, snatched up a pil-low, and covered herself.

"That's a nice nightgown," Fairer Than further com-mented. Despite herself, her mouth crept up into a wolf-ish smile.

"How did —? We have — how did you cross our garden," Bunny demanded.

"And not trip your bluebells alert system?" Fairer Than supplied helpfully. "I leapt."

"And *why* would you leap over the garden, Fairer Than?"

Fairer Than leaned on the sill. She no longer felt wolf-ish. "I wanted to wish you a 'good night,'" she said, sincere.

The silence that greeted her desire nearly worried her. Bunny's gaze seemed to process a string of thoughts.

Fairer Than watched the succession, fascinated. Wit-nessing such emotions was rare in the gaze of faeries.

Bunny brought out her wand from behind the pillow.

"Well, now you have," she said, and twirled her wand in Fairer Than's direction. Fairer Than looked down, startled. Her elbows rested on air. Bunny had shifted her windowsill and the cracked wall to another dimension. Fairer Than's toes slipped off the timber.

"Since you're part-dragon, I doubt the fall will hurt," Bunny said as Fairer Than fell back. Fairer Than's view tilted and she saw the night sky. She rapidly descended.

Boom

Fairer Than, being more solid (and dense of body) than the usual faerie, impacted the garden floor and sent up a cloud of dust and soil. She regained her feet, none the worse for wear, except that she was dirty again. She dusted off her kirtle and looked up.

Bunny gazed down, inscrutable, and still clutched her pillow.

"I feel you like me, Bunny," Fairer Than called up. If she had a heart (which she'd long ago hidden) still in her chest, she believed it would have lightened, feeling gay. Instead, its shadow did so. Fairer Than grinned.

"You've yet to say you don't," she added.

Tinkle

Fairer Than froze, then looked down. Her skirt had touched a bluebell's flower.

A horseshoe swung towards her in the darkness, tied to a string. The iron made her teeth hurt and her skin crawl. A pounding began beneath her skull. Fairer Than grimaced and pulled back.

"Ergh," she said.

"*Yaaaaa!*" Aunt Hauntie and Weirdie yelled. Hauntette brandished the fishing pole the horseshoe swung from. Weirdette, in hair rollers and flimsy gown, shook bird-boned arms in the air, fists clenched.

"Shoo! Shoo!" they cried in unison, and advanced on

Fairer Than.

≈

Bunny watched as her aunties forced Fairer Than to slowly back out of the garden, brushing bluebells and ringing the blossoms as she did so. Fairer Than held up her hands to placate the little old ladies.

"Now, now," she said.

The aunties backed Fairer Than into the low stone fence, where she tripped, flipped over the wall backwards, and fell outside their garden. Fairer Than exclaimed in surprise.

Hauntette whooped and Weirdette snorted, giggling madly.

"And stay out," they cried.

Bunny reluctantly smiled. She appreciated that Fairer Than had made a big enough show to give her aunties an inflated sense of victory.

With a wand wave, Bunny restored her wall and windowsill from where she'd sent it. But the wall crack needed to be repaired conventionally. A magical fix, at least at Bunny's skill level, would only be a glamour. She put out her lights and went to bed. She blew a kiss to Dean's framed name, and set her worn stuffed rabbit aside.

Faeries, she thought before falling asleep.

Her curtains blew, and she dreamed.

She looked up at Fairer Than, crowned in roses and astride a dragon steed. Fairer Than bent to meet her gaze, and her gown and impossibly long, red mantle of hair seemed to engulf Bunny. Bunny's heart expanded with love. Joy vibrated; rose petals fell. At Bunny's wrist, Fairer Than had tied a silk handkerchief, a love token from a lady, fairest of them all.

"Are you happy, Bunny?" Fairer Than spoke, and she was no longer astride her beast but holding Bunny in her arms. The embrace was hot; a hearth Bunny could forever dwell in.

"Oh very, very," Bunny said. She was the very shape of a heart. Fairer Than's hand brushed the pearls in Bunny's hair, and then her face.

"You have nothing to fear. I'll always keep you safe," Fairer Than said. "And we'll have lots of children."

"Really?" Bunny looked at her love, and somewhere in the depths of her soul, a sad, small truth winked out, put to final rest.

"Really." Fairer Than's gaze encompassed. Bunny saw nothing but determination, will, and dedication, wrapped in fiery confidence.

"*For am I not DRAGON?*" Fairer Than spoke.

"Oh, Fairer Than! I love children!"

"And I love you." Fairer Than's mouth descended.

Bunny lay beneath her as they kissed, feeling flesh, heat, and safety, and smelled only amber and roses.

Bunny abruptly woke, pulling herself up from the bed.

"*Goddess*," she uttered. "Oh Goddess." She covered her face.

As the dream faded, her heart ached for what went missing.

"All right," she whispered. "I do like you."

CHAPTER NINE

Dreams held some truths, and even before the rationality of the waking day, Bunny couldn't deny what the dream told: she wanted the comfort of warmth, safety, and a future promising many children. But she was a girl yet to finish high school. There was plenty of time to consider those things. What she needed was to face her desire for Fairer Than.

Bunny sat on the curb outside Haunt High's gates, the tower striking the time for school's end. While students ran by—a wolf boy on all fours and a ghost girl, shimmering—Bunny waited for Dean. Since Blanchet and Pippita had already gone on to Shivers, Bunny allowed herself to sink into the sobriety they would have questioned. She belatedly noticed when Dean stood behind her; her girlfriend might have been standing there for a long while.

"Hey beautiful," Dean said, grinning.

Bunny sprang to her feet, the gloom in her heart fleeing. How could she doubt love when Dean made her feel that happy?

~

"Yesterday it was just me and Blanchet at the soda shop," Bunny chatted as she and Dean strolled down Little Salem's streets, holding hands. "Oh, and Pippita had to be a real pain, so I turned her into a chicken! I gave her an easy way to change back. She only has to eat a worm. What else? I helped Aunt Agoosta with her tarts, and I really think they'll be a hit at the witches' bingo." Dean chuckled. "What?" Bunny demanded. "What's so funny?"

"You haven't stopped talking since I picked you up after school," Dean said, grinning.

"I haven't seen you for almost two days! I missed you." Bunny stifled a yawn.

"And now I'm boring you?" Dean teased.

"No…I haven't been sleeping well." Bunny looked across the street to where a two-headed mother walked with her stroller.

"Oh yeah? What's keeping you up?"

Bunny didn't answer. At the newsstand across, Fairer Than leaned against the stand's wall. She held open a copy of *Young Witch* magazine. She watched Bunny and Dean walk. Her heavy-lidded gaze met Bunny's.

Bunny moved closer to Dean and took her arm. When she glanced at Dean, Dean was looking across the street as well, her gaze narrowing.

~

Dean took Bunny for burgers, and in the bustle and gaiety of the soda shop, Bunny mustered cheer. Dean didn't seem curious or bothered by Fairer Than's presence earlier. Yet while the jukebox played and their school friends danced, Bunny tried to figure out how to bring the subject up. The thought of Dean's likely reaction always halted her.

You're not tough enough to take on Fairer Than. It was not something Dean would want to hear. Ever. No matter how Bunny might explain Fairer Than's interest, the imagined scenario always seemed to end the same: Dean would immediately run out to challenge Fairer Than, and Fairer Than would kill Dean.

Perhaps death was an exaggeration, but Bunny had never heard lore where dragons did anything by halves. All her recent magic study was for naught; magical brawn was not needed against Fairer Than. What appeased or defeated dragons was cleverness, but Dean was not the sort to woo or trick greater beings with wit, cunning, or charm, thereby gaining a concession or favor.

If Blanchet were my girlfriend and had wanted to confront Fairer Than, she'd know how to use her brain, Bunny thought sourly.

Dean glanced at the diner's entrance when more kids walked in. It was an automatic response, checking to see if members of the rival werewolf gang were visiting. If Fairer Than walked through the door next, what then?

Bunny feigned a yawn—one that grew into a genuinely big one. Dean noticed.

"Mind if we call it a night?" Bunny suggested.

Dean was solicitous, as always. When they stepped out of Shivers, she gave Bunny her leather jacket to wear as a chill had entered the evening air. At least that was what

Bunny felt.

"The cold could never bother me, anyways," Dean said as she helped Bunny into the jacket. It was true; she was undead. Though heat was something Dean enjoyed, like a hot bath, it was not a necessity. The jacket, cool to the touch, smelled of leather and Dean's soap. While Dean fetched her bike, Bunny tested the air with her breath; no mist formed.

She was rendered cold, perhaps, by what was foremost on her mind. On the motorcycle ride home and while clinging to Dean's back, she faced a consideration: she could break up with Dean.

Fairer Than would be assuaged, Dean would be devastated but alive, and Bunny might get an answer to what her soul whispered about only in dreams.

The forest trees that they sped past seemed to stretch and reveal hollows in their trunks, forming sad and gaping faces.

～

"I'll see you tomorrow night, Dean," Bunny said as she stood by her front garden gate. The Queer Youth dance was tomorrow. She gave Dean her jacket.

"Okay—oh wait! I forgot something." Dean ran back to her bike. She had parked it away from the house, as the aunties were adamant that her foul and noisy machine not make tracks before the cottage. She fetched something from the saddlebag, and then ran back to Bunny.

"Here you go." Dean handed Bunny a wooden ladle, the tag still attached. "Is this the right kind?"

"A—an oak wood ladle?" Surprised, Bunny accepted the gift.

"Yeah, you said Aunt Hauntie threw the last one at a werewolf, right?"

"Yes, but—Dean, how did you know to get this kind?" By its weight and fit, Bunny knew she held a warmly crafted piece in her hand. The ladle was handmade, and not a casual or modest choice.

Dean shrugged. "I didn't. I asked Fausta to choose for me since she cooks too." She leaned and quickly pecked Bunny on the cheek. "Gotta go! See you tomorrow!"

Dean ran away with a vampire's speed as two garlic missiles zipped past Bunny.

"Ya missed, Hauntette!" Weirdette hollered from the cottage's window. "Oi, more ammo!"

Bunny held the ladle to herself and watched Dean go.

Bunny did not show the ladle to her aunts or drop it off in the kitchen. She brought it up to her room, sat on her bed, and looked at it in her hands when her cat walked in.

Inky crossed the room, her tail in the air, and hopped into Bunny's lap. Bunny stroked Inky's back and showed her the ladle.

"Would a faerie give me such a gift?" she asked the cat.

"Of course she would," Inky answered. "And it wouldn't be real. I need clothes."

"Okay. But please bring them back."

Inky hopped to the floor. She walked away, tail high and her petite paws mincing. Then she stopped and shook herself hard.

Her little body expanded and transformed, and the body that then appeared on Bunny's floor became a young woman's. Jet-black in skin and hair and with pale golden eyes, Inky appeared to be in her early twenties. Bunny had never found out her true age. Sometimes, Bunny wished Inky would act the big sister and advise her.

"Why should I? You wouldn't listen to me, anyway," Inky had retorted, and then produced yet another catalog clipping for an outfit she wanted Bunny to make or put on layaway. At least when it came to clothes, Bunny felt she had an older girl's guidance.

Inky arched her back, her nails biting wood. She rose and headed for Bunny's closet.

Bunny had not learned Inky was more than a cat until the last year, when she happened upon Inky in her bedroom trying on shoes—while also wearing one of Bunny's pencil skirts and blouses. She suspected Inky began transforming into her human form once Bunny had matured enough to be the same dress size. Since Inky was a cat, after all, and a very independent one that Bunny had accepted the care of, Bunny didn't mind being convenient.

She abruptly stood up, everything Aunt Agoosta having said of Other-beings becoming clear.

It wouldn't be real...as an intention or a ladle.

She hurried over to her mirror and lit candles. Inky inspected outfits and blithely ignored her.

Blanchet answered her mirror, blinking sleepily.

"I need your help," Bunny said.

CHAPTER TEN

When a girl kisses a girl
she blasts off 'round the world
Aw yeah

A bright moon shone over Okanee Swamp while the music played. Paper skull lanterns gently swung from the cypresses and dangling vines over Queer Youth's dance. A three-girl group in beehive hairdos and A-line dresses sang along with the record player, and couples spun in the clearing. Boys moved with boys, girls with girls, and if the dancers weren't discernible as either sex, it didn't matter. Bunny and Dean danced the Lindy, the Bop, and then the cha-cha. Bunny looked to the forest edge and saw Fairer Than, standing in the shadows. When the music changed to a slower pace and lines formed for the Stroll, Bunny and Dean moved away for the refreshments table.

"I'll be back," Bunny said. Dean wore a white dress

jacket with black lapels and no tie. Bunny ignored the sudden ache in her heart.

"Sure," Dean said, pouring out a cup of punch. Bunny gave her a quick kiss on the cheek.

She slipped away into the forest area where she'd seen Fairer Than last. As she made her way through darkness, the lantern lights and music faded. She brought out a new lipstick, uncapped it, and applied it to her lips.

"Hello, Bunny," Fairer Than said, and she stood in a moonlit clearing by the water.

Bunny came to a stop, her heart beating quickly. She pocketed the lipstick. Fairer Than glanced above to the moon.

"Nice night; much like how we first met," she remarked.

"Now Fairer Than," Bunny said, steeling herself.

"Bunny." Fairer Than neared, her gaze darkly confident, and she smiled. "Why fight it?"

Bunny took a breath. "Why indeed?" She approached.

Fairer Than paused and watched her, receptive.

Bunny stepped passed Fairer Than and while slowly circling, she allowed longing into her gaze. Fairer Than smelled like a place Bunny could dwell in. She locked the thought away.

"Around you, it was hard for me to understand something, even when it was before me, the entire time," she mused.

"What, Bunny?" Fairer Than tolerated the appraisal, seemingly amused, but her tone held uncertainty.

"You are so distracting. With those hips, and breasts… that face, and gorgeous mouth of yours. But the truth remained: why don't I fall into your arms? Why do I resist your charms? Something holds me back, and it's not just my love for Dean."

Bunny completed her circle. She came to a stop before

Fairer Than.

"If I choose you, I'd only be another notch in that belt of yours," she said.

Fairer Than's eyes widened.

"Isn't that true?" Bunny demanded. "Isn't it the truth, Fairer Than?" her fists clenched. "Must I ask a third time?"

"I…I guess I am bad, for a reason," Fairer Than said.

"You're all charms and gestures; beauty and fire." Bunny stepped away. "But no heart, Fairer Than. Good bye." She turned to leave.

"I will not be deterred."

Bunny halted at the sudden ferocity in Fairer Than's voice. When she turned back, fire flickered behind Fairer Than's irises.

"Oh no you don't." Bunny raised a finger. "I'm not something convenient—some good-time girl you can have whenever you want. I am more than that."

"And you are." Fairer Than's gaze and voice seemed to smolder. "Once my eyes are set, must the prize be met, and won. I must have you, Bunny. Convince me that *you* do not want me, and that it's done, or I'll pursue you to the ends of the Twilight World and beyond."

Bunny bristled.

"Come here," Bunny commanded and pointed to the ground at her feet.

Fairer Than started, her intensity interrupted. Subdued, she did as asked. Bunny held Fairer Than's face and kissed her on the lips.

Fairer Than drew back, aghast. Her fist went to her mouth.

"Erm," she said, muffled. "That was…interesting."

"No, that was awful," Bunny said, stern. "*That's* the kind of chemistry we have. And that's all you can expect if you keep this up. It's over, Fairer Than."

Fairer Than stood, out of sorts.

She then pulled Bunny to her.

"Let me try again." Her mouth descended.

"No—" Bunny said, but Fairer Than's lips covered hers.

Dean grabbed Fairer Than, knocking Bunny to the ground. She heaved Fairer Than above her head, then flung her far out into the water.

SPLASH

When Dean looked at Bunny, tears filled Dean's eyes.

"*Dean!*" Bunny cried, struggling to get up. Dean ran away into the forest.

"*DEAN!*"

Only the forest's silence answered.

⁓

The next day, Pippita and Blanchet walked to Shivers.

It was the weekend; no school. In Little Salem, the day was blue-skied and sun-filled, with the occasional hot rod blazing above the town. A flock of winged women flew past. But the mood on the street seemed subdued, as if everyone knew what had happened last night.

"So...did Dean buy your story?" Pippita asked.

Blanchet sighed. "It wasn't a story. I helped Bunny in figuring out a way to deal with Fairer Than. What happened last night was as much my fault as...well, I really don't think Bunny was at fault." She pulled out a lipstick from her bag and showed it to Pippita. "Here's the culprit."

"'Mama Vouloirs's *Repelere* Lip Gloss,'" Pippita read on the label. She grabbed the stick.

"Yeah. One kiss, and it's supposed to repel your unwanted suitor for good." Blanchet sighed again. "If I were in Dean's place? Maybe I'd feel the same—hurt about not being told. And hurt about how Bunny chose to handle it—how I *helped* her handle it. But Bunny's my friend, and I love her, too. I can't blame her. We *are* talking about dragons."

"We sure are. *Rarr.* Why isn't Bunny cuddly with Fairer Than again?" Pippita said.

"*Don't ask.*"

Pippita pursed her lips and applied the lipstick. "Mama Vouloirs should have test-marketed this on dragon lips." She smacked her lips as they entered Shivers.

Bunny sat at a window booth, staring sightlessly into the street. She'd rather be home crying her eyes out. But Blanchet wanted to mend things as quickly as possible— or at least attempt to mend things, feeling that she was to blame. Either way, Bunny would know for certain how much damage she'd wrought.

"I am super...super sorry to say this, but you need to know if it's really done," Blanchet had told her.

Bunny waited. Supposedly, Dean had agreed to come meet her.

When Bunny saw Blanchet arrive down the walk with only Pippita, she tried hard not to despair and blinked her tears away. Her friends entered.

"Oh no you don't," she heard Blanchet say to Pippita, and her friend steered Pippita away from Bunny's booth towards the counter stools. Bunny was grateful. Pippita was not so malicious as to willfully hurt her more, but she was a demon, and like many of the Other-beings, they saw things the way humans could not. Bunny was not ready for any frank and painful pearls of wisdom.

A sprite hovered before her.

Bunny blinked, uncomprehending. His was a worn and

lined face with a limp mohawk. He wore leather pants and steel-toed boots.

"Greetings," he said in a raspy voice as his ragged wings fluttered. "M'lady would like to apo—"

SMACK

Dean backhanded the sprite, sending him into the scenic window. The smashed sprite slid down the glass.

Bunny looked up at Dean and saw her puffy eyes.

"We gotta talk," Dean said.

⁓

When Blanchet glanced back to Bunny's booth again, her friend was walking out with Dean.

She and Pippita scurried for the scenic window. They pressed their faces to the glass. Bunny and Dean moved down the walk, away from the scrutiny of the kids in the diner.

"Huh. Dean lucked out," Pippita declared. "If she'd just waited *five* more minutes, this would have been a different story." She pointed across the street and Blanchet looked.

"Yeah, funny how that works," Blanchet said.

"There's still a chance for Dean to blow it," Pippita added, her tone snide.

They pressed more into the glass and stared at the couple.

⁓

Bunny stood on the walk, her and Dean's silence separating them as effectively as the physical distance between them. What could Bunny say that Blanchet hadn't already told Dean? What had hurt the most, that she couldn't heal with the mere word, *sorry*?

And then it struck her, a shower of cold water.

She was not sorry for taking control.

She was only sorry for having hurt Dean by doing so.

Bunny opened her mouth to speak.

"Wait," Dean said. "Let's…" She brought Bunny into a hug. Her arms crushed. The air left Bunny's lungs and she smelled leather and soap.

"You'll say you're sorry," Dean said as she held Bunny tight. "And then I'll say I'm sorry. No matter what's said…I love you, Bunny."

Bunny's breath caught and her tears came.

"I love you too," Bunny whispered.

≈

Mugg winged his way across the street from the diner, his flight path erratic. One eye swelled; an impressive shiner. Before him, his mistress stood within the shade of trees, a forearm resting against a tree trunk. Fairer Than watched the embracing couple he'd left behind.

Mugg alighted on her shoulder and whispered into her ear.

"Ha! Some wreck *this* turned out ta be!" A female sprite exclaimed. She fluttered beside Mugg. "The two are now talking!"

"The bond, nearly broken, *mends* itself, mayhap," A third sprite observed, and he popped up next to the female. The female donned a trumpet blossom: her witch's hat. The male responded by sticking two pine needles into his mouth, simulating fangs.

"Oh Deano," the female said, her eyes large and luminous, and she clasped her hands. "Thou art my *true love*, verily!"

"Though I be wrecked by these past events, I'll *still* be

your undead, baby!" the male lisped in response.

The two abandoned their playacting and burst into raucous laughter.

"'Lo, up there!" the female sprite called as she plopped
down on Fairer Than's bosom. "Dark One! Let us find a
new victim. An easier mark than some pretty-pretty that
can see through thy charms!" She and the male sprite then
flew up to tug on Fairer Than's hair, hoping to budge her.

After a while of pulling, the sprites looked at each other.

"Could it *be*?" the female said.

"*Dare* we think it?" the male replied.

"Might Fairer Than the Fairest of all Faeries—*be in
love*?" they cried.

They departed, hooting and hollering.

Mugg sat down on Fairer Than's shoulder and joined
his lady in watching Bunny. Fairer Than stood, as silent
and still as the trees, and recalled the greens, browns, and
grays reflected in Bunny's eyes; windows to the vulner-
able and beautiful. Such soul drew Fairer Than. It was the
song of a woman's self that she'd forgotten.

And her heart's shadow responded.

"Surprise," Fairer Than softly said.

The end.

Next:
Vampire versus Faerie
in
Hot Roddin' To Hell

And now~
turn the page
to see
how
I draw
Bunny & Fairer Than.

(Break Time, Two . . .)

Read more in
Charm School Graphique Vol 1
and
Charm School Digital No 1-9

More from Elizabeth:
Hot Roddin' To Hell: A Charm School Novella Vol 2
Body Chase: A Charm School Novella Vol 3

The Dark Victorian: Risen Vol 1
The Dark Victorian: Bones Vol 2
Ice Demon: A Dark Victorian Penny Dread Vol 1
Medusa: A Dark Victorian Penny Dread Vol 2
Sundark: An Elle Black Penny Dread Vol 1
Poison Garden: An Elle Black Penny Dread Vol 2
Monster Stalker: A Darquepunk Novel Vol 1
Bloody Nike: A Darquepunk Novel Vol 2

Author's Notes

Charm School, the comic book:
Charm School the comic book was originally published by Slave Labor Graphics (SLG Publishing) from 1999 to 2003. Written and drawn by me, there were nine issues, with a tenth and final issue long promised. Bunny first appeared in the comic book short story, *Bunny the Good Li'l Teen Witch*, published in *Action Girl Comics* #13 in 1997, also by SLG Publishing.

Sequential art versus only words:

In novelizing *Charm School*'s first story arc, "The Wrecking Faerie," there were story aspects I could finally flesh out and go deeper into, plus add more scenes. But some visual aspects from the comic book were lost. It's easier in sequential art to draw in extraneous visuals—silent, independent background stories—to entertain and inform the reader while the main story goes on. During the cafeteria sequence where Pippita regales Bunny and Blanchet with dragon tales, certain epic scenes are illustrated to emphasize her words. In fiction, I succeeded in having Bunny visualize three out of the four that appeared in the comic book.

And while Pippita, Bunny, and Blanchet discuss Fairer Than in the cafeteria, background characters are going about their lives: a wolf boy and a monster boy toss someone's irate skull around. Mummy boy argues with his girlfriend via a crystal ball borrowed from a disgruntled Goth witch girl. Cyclops girl is doing her homework. I managed to work some of them back into the fiction by moving the activity to when Bunny prepares her broom for the ride home. But background events or characters depicted at the Q-Youth meeting, vampires' ball, or at the dance were pretty much discarded.

Another thing that couldn't go into the novelization were my A-Girl Easter eggs. For anyone familiar with my small press zine comic, *The Adventures of A-Girl!*, published during the early '90's, you'd know that A-Girl made background cameos or product appearances in *Charm School*'s panels. For example, in *Charm School* #3, A-Girl appears as a button on a flaming person's jacket front while that person watches Bunny and Dean dance.

Despite losing extraneous visuals, the fiction is enhanced. One comic book panel of water faeries or of Bunny sitting in silence holding a ladle can expand and deepen with the written word. Inky the cat, who's not in the comic book, can now be introduced. Sequential art, by its nature, makes the reader's imagination participate and provide the unspoken details. The reader chooses the words for Bunny's silence. In long fiction, I've decided to choose, though I'm certain there were elegant solutions around that.

Charm School was published on good old-fashioned pulp paper, limited to only 24 pages an issue. This was before web and digital comics, so the story had to get all points across in those 24 pages. The novelization is possibly a more mature animal. I'm very happy to bring that to realization.

About The Author

Elizabeth Watasin is the author of the Gothic steampunk series *The Dark Victorian*, The *Elle Black Penny Dreads*, the *Darquepunk* series, and the creator/artist of the indie comics series *Charm School*, which was nominated for a Gaylactic Spectrum Award. A twenty year veteran of animation and comics, her credits include thirteen feature films, such as *Beauty and the Beast, Aladdin, The Lion King,* and *The Princess and the Frog,* and writing for *Disney Adventures* magazine. She lives in Los Angeles with her black cat named Draw, busy bringing readers uncanny heroines in shilling shockers, preternatural fantasies, and adventuress tales.

Follow the news of her latest projects at A-Girl Studio.
www.a-girlstudio.com
amazon.com/author/elizabethwatasin
www.facebook.com/ElizabethWatasinX
twitter.com/ewatasin

ELIZABETH WATASIN

The DARK
VICTORIAN

BONES